Sammy the Shy Kitten

Other titles by Holly Webb

The Snow Bear

The Reindeer Girl

The Winter Wolf

The Storm Leopards

Animal Stories:

Lost in the Snow

Alfie all Alone

Lost in the Storm

Sam the Stolen Puppy

Max the Missing Puppy

Sky the Unwanted Kitten

Timmy in Trouble

Ginger the Stray Kitten

Harry the Homeless Puppy

Buttons the Runaway Puppy

Alone in the Night

Ellie the Homesick Puppy

Jess the Lonely Puppy

Misty the Abandoned Kitten

Oscar's Lonely Christmas

Lucy the Poorly Puppy

Smudge the Stolen Kitten

The Rescued Puppy

The Kitten Nobody Wanted

The Lost Puppy

The Frightened Kitten

The Secret Puppy

The Abandoned Puppy

The Missing Kitten

The Puppy Who was Left Behind

The Kidnapped Kitten

The Scruffy Puppy

The Brave Kitten

The Forgotten Puppy

The Secret Kitten

A Home for Molly

Maisie Hitchins:

The Case of the Stolen Sixpence

The Case of the Vanishing Emerald

The Case of the Phantom Cat

The Case of the Feathered Mask

The Case of the Secret Tunnel

The Case of the Spilled Ink

The Case of the Blind Beetle

The Case of the Weeping Mermaid

Sammy the Shy Kitten

Holly Webb
Illustrated by Sophy Williams

For Daisy

www.hollywebbanimalstories.com

STRIPES PUBLISHING
An imprint of Little Tiger Press
1 The Coda Centre, 189 Munster Road,
London SW6 6AW

A paperback original
First published in Great Britain in 2016

Text copyright © Holly Webb, 2016
Illustrations copyright © Sophy Williams, 2016

ISBN: 978-1-84715-648-8

The right of Holly Webb and Sophy Williams to be
identified as the author and illustrator of this work
respectively has been asserted by them in accordance
with the Copyright, Designs and Patents Act, 1988.

A CIP catalogue record for this book is available
from the British Library.

Printed and bound in the UK.

10 9 8 7 6 5 4 3 2 1

Chapter One

"See you later, Mum!" Emma waved as her mum drove off down the bumpy lane that led to Ivy Bank Stables. She was looking forward to seeing her best friend Keira, but she would see most of her riding-class friends at school on Monday. Really she wanted to say hello to the ponies, and the cats that lived at the stables, too.

Emma didn't always see the cats – they were all very shy, almost wild. She wasn't even sure how many of them there were, no one was. Liz, who owned the riding school, said she thought there were five. But Emma was almost certain there were six, and that the skinny ginger cat was actually two skinny ginger cats. Once she thought she'd seen him strolling along the roof of the feed store only seconds after he'd been sunbathing out by the paddock.

Liz put down food and water for the cats, but only once a day. Mostly they lived by hunting. They earned their keep by getting rid of the mice and rats that sniffed around the stables after the horses' feed.

"Hello, Sparky," Emma murmured, going to pat the nose of the grey she usually rode in her class. The pony snorted and put his nose over the half-door of his stall. He nudged happily at her hand, searching for an apple or a carrot. He knew Emma always brought him treats. Emma giggled and brought out a piece of carrot. "And I've got Polos for afterwards, if you're good," she whispered. "But don't tell the others. I'll just go and let Liz know I'm here, then I'll be back to tack you up."

Emma looked around hopefully for the cats as she went over to find Liz, but none of them seemed to be around. She crouched down and peeped behind the tulips in the little flowerbed in front of the office. The ginger cat (one of the ginger cats, anyway) practically lived in the flowerbed, and sometimes he'd let her stroke him. Sure enough, there he was, curled up tightly into a stripy ball. He opened one yellow-green eye and glared at her. He obviously didn't want to be petted.

Emma sighed and put her head round the office door.

"Hi, Liz. Mum dropped me off a bit early so I could say hello to the ponies. I wanted to see if I could stroke Tiggy, too, but I can't find her."

Tiggy was Emma's favourite of the stable cats – she was black and had longer fur than the others, with a thick bushy tail. She spent a lot of time lying in the sun and grooming, cleaning bits of hay out of her pretty fur.

Liz had looked up, smiling, when she first spotted Emma, but now her smile faded. "I haven't actually seen her for a couple of days. I'm starting to get a bit worried. I know the cats aren't really pets and they wander around all over the place, but usually Tiggy's the friendliest of them all. She doesn't disappear like Susie and Ginger, and she's almost always in the yard."

Emma nodded, frowning. "I don't think I've ever been to the stables and not seen her."

9

"She's been so hungry lately, but she hasn't come to the food bowls," Liz sighed. "I'm sure I'd have noticed her."

Emma glanced out at the bowls. Liz kept them by the bench in the yard, which had a wooden canopy built over it. It meant that the food stayed dry and the nervous cats didn't have to go inside for it. Emma smiled as she saw Susie, a thin little tabby, slinking over to see if there was anything left. But then she turned back towards Liz.

"So … Tiggy hasn't eaten anything for two days?" she asked anxiously.

Liz shook her head. "Not from here, I don't think. She's a good mouser, so maybe she's just been hunting more. I wish I'd seen her around, though."

Emma nibbled her bottom lip. "At least the stables is quite far from the main road," she said slowly. Her Auntie Grace's cat, Whisky, had been hit by a car a couple of years ago and had broken his leg really badly. He was better now, but Auntie Grace hated him going round the front of the house. She always tried to tempt him back inside if she saw him sitting on the front wall.

Liz smiled at her. "Exactly. I'm probably worrying over nothing."

She didn't make Emma feel much better, though. Where could Tiggy have gone?

"Anyway," Liz said briskly. "We should get on. The others will be here by now." She got up and put an arm round Emma's shoulders. "Don't worry. You know what cats are like – especially these half-wild ones. We'll get all upset and then she'll stroll in without a care in the world."

Emma giggled. But she wished that Tiggy would stroll in *now*.

Maybe it was because she was thinking about Tiggy, or maybe it was just a bad day, but nothing seemed to go right for Emma that morning. Tacking up Sparky took ages. He wouldn't stay still – he jittered and sidestepped and nibbled at her jacket. Then he nearly trod on her foot as she lead him over to the outdoor arena.

"Are you OK?" her friend Keira asked, as she finally managed to get to the gate. "You look a bit stressed."

"Sparky's just being … Sparky," Emma sighed. "He's lovely when he wants to be, but…"

Keira grinned and nodded. "I know. Maybe he's just excited."

"He's always excited!"

"Are you ready, girls?" Liz came over to check that their girths were tight. "Now, the jumps are a bit higher than last week, but you're all perfectly capable of clearing these fences. Just don't let the ponies try to take them too fast."

Emma nodded a little nervously. She really did love Sparky. The gentler ponies, like Keira's mount Jasmine, just didn't have as much personality as the bouncy grey. But she had a feeling that trying to keep Sparky calm and collected wouldn't be that easy today. Luckily they were going first so Sparky wouldn't get bored. The thrill of riding a fast, eager pony took over as they set off, and Emma had a huge smile on her face by the time they'd cleared the second jump.

Then somehow everything went wrong. Perhaps Sparky decided he didn't like the look of the new rainbow-striped rails that Liz had used for the third jump. He slid round to the left of the jump instead of going over. Emma did her best to encourage him on, but Sparky was determined – he swerved sideways round the jump, and Emma felt herself slipping out of the saddle. There was a horrible, slow moment when she knew she was falling. Then all of a sudden she was on the ground, with her ankle twisted and aching, and Sparky standing over her. He looked quite apologetic.

"Emma!" Liz came hurrying over, catching Sparky's reins and handing them to Keira. "Hold on to him, Keira, while I check Emma's all right."

"I don't think I rode him at it straight enough," Emma said, wincing as she tried to stand. "Ow, my ankle…"

Liz gently felt the ankle through Emma's boot. "I don't think it's swelling up. Do you want me to call Alex and get him to bring you an ice pack?"

"It's OK. Sorry I messed up…"

"No, you were doing really well. It looked like Sparky just decided against that jump. Can you put any weight on your ankle?"

"I think so." Emma blinked, trying not to cry.

Liz helped her up. "Are you sure you're all right?"

Emma nodded. "It was just a bit of a shock…"

"Look, sit down on the bench. We'll tie Sparky up to the fence, and I'll come and check on you again in a bit."

Liz went back to schooling the others over the jumps, and Emma watched from the side of the arena, gently rubbing her ankle. It was starting to feel a bit better already. She clapped as Keira jumped Jasmine clear, and her friend waved at her.

Emma stood up and leaned on the fence, testing the weight on her ankle. It was definitely feeling better. She was just thinking about asking Liz if it was OK to untie Sparky again, when she heard a strange squeaky noise behind her. She glanced round. The outdoor arena was next to a shabby old barn that Liz was planning to get rid of, so they could make the arena bigger. It was divided up into stalls for horses, but they weren't used any more. The noise was definitely coming from in there, though. Emma limped curiously over to the door – that was falling apart, too, a couple of the boards had rotted away at the bottom.

She lifted the latch, pushed open the door and looked round it cautiously. Maybe a bird had got trapped inside – she didn't like the idea of it flapping out at her. But there was no bird, only the raspy creak of the door – and then that tiny, breathy little squeak again. Emma walked in slowly, following the noise. It sounded like it was coming from the stall at the end.

Emma stopped and peered round the open half-door. There was still some straw on the floor, piled up in the corner. The squeaking was coming from over there, and for one horrible moment Emma wondered if it was a rat.

Then a dark head looked up over the straw, and Emma laughed in surprise.

"Tiggy!" she said, keeping her voice low. "Liz is really worried about you, you know. What are you doing in here?"

Tiggy eyed her cautiously, her ears flickering, and Emma frowned. She'd never heard Tiggy squeak like that before, she realized. And there was something else in the straw – something small and wriggly and dark. Actually there were several somethings…

"Oh! Tiggy, have you…?" Emma stepped closer, trying to lean over the door just a little so she could see without scaring the cat. She'd completely forgotten about her twisted ankle now. "You have! You've had kittens!"

Chapter Two

The kittens were so sweet, squirming around over each other in the straw and nuzzling at their mother. Tiggy glared suspiciously at Emma for a moment. Then she obviously decided that it was safe to ignore her and went back to licking her babies all over. Emma tried not to giggle. It looked as though Tiggy was determined that they would be just as beautifully groomed as she was.

"So that's why you were really hungry. It's OK, Tiggy. I won't come any closer." Emma hung on to the door post, counting. "It's three, isn't it?" she whispered. "Two black kittens and one grey tabby. I ought to go and tell the others…" But she didn't want to leave just yet. The kittens were so little Emma wondered when they'd been born.

"I'd better go and tell Liz," she said at last, slowly backing away. "Don't go anywhere, will you…" She had read about mother cats picking up their kittens in their mouths to move them if she thought they weren't safe. She hoped she hadn't scared Tiggy into doing anything like that. But Tiggy didn't look too worried. "I'll get Liz to find you some food, too," Emma added, her eyes widening. "Oh, Tiggy, you must be starving!"

As soon as she was out of sight of Tiggy, Emma whisked round and limped out of the barn as fast as she could.

Liz waved when she saw her and hurried over. "Emma! I just noticed that you'd disappeared. How's your ankle? It doesn't look like it's swollen."

Emma shook her head, grinning at Liz. "No, it feels nearly better now. And I've found Tiggy."

"Oh, that's brilliant! Where was she? Is she all right?"

Emma giggled. "She's more than all

right. You have to come and see!"

"I need to watch the others. Can you show me at the end?" Liz glanced between Emma and the rest of the class, and Emma realized that of course she couldn't leave them riding without an instructor.

"It's OK. I don't think Tiggy's going anywhere." Emma folded her arms and glanced back at the barn.

Liz sighed. "I hope this is worth all the suspense, Emma! Come on, you'd better catch up with the others. Sparky looks very sorry for himself."

Sparky did seem to think that he'd been missing out. He brightened up as he saw Emma and jumped two clear rounds with her as soon as he was allowed back into the ring.

"You monster!" Emma told him
affectionately, as she patted his nose
afterwards. "You can have a Polo –
here. But I don't think you deserve
it. Why didn't you do that first time
round, instead of tipping me off?"
Sparky whiffled up the Polo from her
hand eagerly, and Emma smiled.

"I suppose if I hadn't fallen, I wouldn't have found the kittens. Oh, look, Liz is waving. It's the end of the lesson now – I can't wait for her to see them." She hugged Sparky round the neck and started to walk him back to the gate where the others were waiting. "I'm not showing you, though. I wouldn't trust you not to put your massive great clumpy feet on those kittens."

"What are you so excited about?" Keira asked, as she led Jasmine over towards Emma and Sparky.

"I found Tiggy! Liz hadn't seen her for a couple of days – she was getting worried. You have to come and see!"

Keira looked at her doubtfully. "Sorry, Emma. You know I'm scared of cats."

"I forgot! Sorry, I was just so excited." She bit her lip, not wanting Keira to miss out on the secret. But she knew her friend was especially frightened of the half-wild cats at the stables. "Come here." She leaned over to whisper in Keira's ear. "Tiggy's had kittens. In the old barn! Don't tell Liz yet, OK?"

Keira smiled. "Now I get why you're so excited. Are they cute?" She sounded a little bit wistful, as though she wished she wasn't so nervous around cats.

"I only saw them from a distance, but they were gorgeous. Are you sure you don't want just a little look?"

Keira shook her head. "Tiggy's so jumpy..."

Liz came up behind them. "Are you going to show me this big secret now?"

Emma nodded eagerly, and Keira laughed. "She can't wait – I'm surprised she hasn't told everybody already! Here, I'll lead Sparky back."

Emma handed over the reins and hurried Liz along to the barn door. "Be really quiet!" she whispered, putting a finger up to her lips. Then she led the way inside, tiptoeing over the dusty floor.

"Where is she?" Liz hissed, and then she gasped as Emma pulled her sleeve and pointed into the stall. "Kittens! Oh, wow, I never even thought of that!"

"Three of them," Emma said, beaming. "Aren't they beautiful? Can we put down some food for Tiggy in here? I bet she's really hungry."

Liz nodded. "Yes, definitely. I'll go and get her some now. Gosh, three more cats. That's a lot…"

Emma looked up at her worriedly. "I hadn't thought about that."

Liz made a face. "Well, they are lovely, but I'm not sure how many more cats we can look after, to be honest. We've already got five. I suppose I should have expected this to happen, but none of them have had kittens till now. Probably we should have got them neutered, but they're all so shy. It was a nightmare the one time I had to take Susie to the vet because she'd been in a fight. She was really tricky to catch, and she hated being in the car."

"So..." Emma swallowed – her mouth had gone dry with excitement. When she spoke again, her voice sounded oddly squeaky. "If the kittens couldn't stay here, would you want to find homes for them?"

Liz nodded slowly. "That would be perfect, wouldn't it? Nice homes where they'd be properly looked after."

Emma gazed thoughtfully at the wriggling bundles of fur. "I didn't think of them being pets," she murmured. "I thought they'd be a bit wild, like Tiggy."

Liz shook her head. "I think it's to do with how much they get used to people when they're little. Tiggy and Susie and the others are half-wild because they've never had a proper indoor home or spent much time around people. But it doesn't mean it has to be the same with these little ones."

Emma nodded. That made sense.

"How are you going to find them homes?" she said. "Would you just ... ask people if they wanted them?"

Liz smiled at Emma. "I suppose so. Are you thinking you'd like a kitten? What would your mum and dad say?"

"I don't know." Emma sighed. "But I can ask. I love the idea of taming a little wild kitten!"

Liz snorted. "I wouldn't put it that way to your mum, Emma. She'd worry about you getting your fingers bitten off. Come on, let's go and find Tiggy something to eat."

Chapter Three

"Dad!" Emma ran over to the car where her dad was waiting and flung her arms around his waist. "You'll never guess what happened!"

Her dad blinked at her in surprise. "Did Sparky behave himself for once?"

Emma shook her head and laughed. "Nope, actually he was really tricksy and I fell off. But I'm OK! It's Tiggy

– she's had three kittens, and I found them!"

"That is exciting! Are they really small?"

"I think they're only a day or two old," Emma explained. "Liz said Tiggy had disappeared for a couple of days, so I guess she went off to hide and make herself a little nest. The kittens are teensy – only about this big." She held her hands apart to show him. "Do you want to come and see?"

Dad wrinkled his nose. "I'd love to – but what about Tiggy? Isn't she really shy? If loads of people start tramping past her kittens, she might get upset."

Emma nodded. "I know. But Liz said that seeing as I found them, I can take some food back for Tiggy. You could come with me. Liz has made her a special treat – she found a bit of fish in the freezer. She reckons Tiggy deserves it!"

Dad grinned. "I haven't seen any tiny kittens for years – not since my cat Bella had kittens when I was about your age."

"Did she?" Emma looked surprised. "Didn't you have her neutered, then?"

"She was a stray that Granny May

adopted," Dad explained. "Well, she adopted us, really. She was sitting on the front doorstep one day when we came home from school. We hadn't even got as far as taking her to the vet, to be honest. We were just getting used to having a cat when the kittens arrived. We had her neutered after that… One litter of kittens was fun, but your gran didn't want to find homes for any more."

"You're so lucky," Emma sighed. "I wish we had kittens. Or a grown-up cat – I wouldn't mind." She gave her dad a sideways look. "Dad, if you really like cats, why don't we have one?"

Her dad looked thoughtful. "Well, it would have been tricky when me and Mum were both working full-time.

But I suppose now we've changed our shifts around we could…" Emma's parents both worked at the local hospital. "I don't know what your mum would think, though, Ems. She's never had a cat."

"I don't see how anybody could not like a tiny little kitten," Emma said coaxingly.

"Perhaps because it'll turn into a great big cat clawing the sofa? You know your mum likes everything really tidy in the house."

"A cat could be tidy…" Emma said hopefully. "Oh, Liz has got the food, look!" Liz was standing by the car-park gate, holding a couple of bowls. Emma grabbed her dad's arm, hauling him after her.

"We'll be really careful," she told
Liz, as she took the food bowl. "Oh,
you've got some water, too. I was going
to ask you about that."

Emma's dad took the water bowl
and followed her across the yard to
the old barn. "I can hear them rustling
about," he whispered to Emma, as they
tiptoed over to the stall.

Tiggy was looking anxious, and she
half stood up as Emma and her dad

came to the door of the stall. The kittens squeaked a little and shifted around in the straw nest as their mother moved. Emma ducked her head, trying to see the kittens without staring at Tiggy – she knew from a cat programme she'd seen on TV that cats didn't like to make eye contact sometimes. "It's OK," she whispered. "We brought you some delicious food. Fish – can you smell it?"

She was sure that Tiggy's whiskers flickered, and the fluffy cat was definitely eyeing the bowls.

"I'll put the food here." Emma crouched down and stretched out her arm, trying to get the bowl into the stall without scaring Tiggy. "And Dad's got you some water, too." She glanced across at her dad.

"Can you see the kittens? Look, they haven't even got their eyes open!"

The kittens wriggled and made tiny mewing noises, calling for Tiggy to feed them. They were like little furry balloons, Emma thought, all plump and squidgy. Their fur was still quite short and fine, so the pink skin showed through on their tummies and paws, and their tails were almost as thin as string.

"I wish we could stay and watch," she murmured to Dad, as she edged away, still crouching. "But Tiggy might not want to eat while we're here because it'll mean leaving the kittens."

"I know, she is looking a bit worried," Dad agreed. "I love that little tabby. It looks like it's going to have great silver and black stripes. But they're all cute."

"I like that one, too," Emma whispered, giving the kittens one last look from the doorway. "That's the sort of cat I've always imagined having."

Snuggled in the straw, the kittens cheeped faintly, and blundered their way over towards their mother and her milk. They were so little that food and warmth were the only things

they understood. They heard the soft
vibrations of Emma's voice, and her
dad's, but only Tiggy understood that
Emma had brought her food and
water, and had kept her distance from
the precious kittens.

"The kitten of one of those cats at
the stables?" Emma's mum asked
doubtfully. "I don't think that's a
very good idea, Emma. I know they
look beautiful, but none of them are
friendly. They're all half-wild. I don't
think we want a cat like that." She put
the salad on the kitchen table and sat
down. "It isn't that I don't want us
to have a pet, but we've never had a

cat before. Shouldn't it be somebody who really knows what they're doing looking after kittens like those?"

"But there isn't anybody who knows!" Emma tried to argue. "Liz would be really pleased if we wanted to adopt one, I know she would. You should see him, Mum, the little grey tabby kitten. He's got white paws and white under his chin. His nose is all pink and soft because he's so small."

Mum smiled at her. "He sounds lovely, Emma. But a kitten like that might be a lot of work. Maybe we could find one from somewhere else?"

Emma looked desperately at her dad. She ought to be delighted – Mum had never said anything about being able to get a cat before. Emma knew that she was lucky to have her riding lessons – she'd never thought they'd be able to have a pet at home, too. But now she didn't want just any cat, she wanted to help those little kittens at the stables.

She'd always felt sorry for the stable cats, not having proper homes to go to. They didn't seem to mind – they curled up together in the stalls, and Liz put food out for them – but it wasn't like a lovely warm basket by the radiator, or sleeping at the end of someone's bed. She didn't want the kittens to grow up wild like their mother, even though Tiggy was gorgeous.

"Let's see what we can find out about taming kittens," Dad suggested. "They *were* very sweet. And I think it's too late to put Emma off them. She's already fallen in love with the little tabby. I wonder if it's a boy or a girl? We didn't get close enough to check."

"I thought he was a boy, just because he looked like he was wearing a little white shirt. But I don't know for sure."

Emma's dad looked over at her mum and she smiled.

"We'll see," Mum said. "I'm not promising anything, but perhaps you could do a bit of research. Find out what we'd have to do…"

"Yes!" Emma squealed. "Oh, Mum, this is so exciting! Please can we hurry up and eat lunch so I can look it all up on the computer."

"Hello, Ivy Bank Stables?"

"Hi, Liz," Emma said, a bit shyly. She'd never rung up the stables before – usually Mum did it if they had to book a lesson.

"Oh! Is that you, Emma? Is everything OK? How's your ankle?"

"It doesn't hurt at all now. I'm just ringing because I've been talking to Mum and Dad about the kittens. I asked if we could adopt one, but my mum's not sure. She says maybe it ought to be somebody who's more experienced with cats."

Emma frowned to herself, trying to remember all the information she and Dad had looked up that afternoon. "But the thing is, if they're going to be rehomed, the kittens need to have lots of contact with people, so they're not shy around humans like Tiggy and the others are. So I was wondering if I could come and spend some time with them."

"Yes, that makes sense," Liz said slowly. "And it's lovely that you want to help look after them, Emma. Of course you can – if your mum and dad are fine with it."

"Oh, they are," Emma told her. She hesitated, and then went on, "I'm really hoping Mum will let me adopt one of the kittens, if I can help tame them.

At the moment she's a bit worried that they'll be too wild. But we've found lots of ways to help with that. Me and Dad have been doing loads of research. It's the little tabby one I really love."

"He's adorable, isn't he? So, is there anything I should be doing? Or the others at the stables?" Liz asked.

"I think just try to spend some time with them. Would it be OK if I came to the stables after school sometimes, as well as for my lessons? The more the kittens get used to people, the better. I'm guessing you want to find homes for the others as well?"

Emma heard Liz sigh down the phone. "Yes, I need to think about that. Perhaps I'll put a notice up on the board outside the stables."

"Oh!" Emma suddenly remembered something she'd read on a website. "There's a charity that'll help with neutering the cats. They'll even come and get them for you! They'll catch them and neuter them for free, and then bring them back."

"Really? That sounds amazing. Could you find their details for me, please?" Liz laughed. "You really are serious about cats, aren't you, Emma?"

Chapter Four

Emma went to the stables whenever
she could get Mum or Dad to drive
her. She spent most of her pocket
money on a cat care book, just in case
she did manage to persuade Mum
to take the tabby kitten home. The
kitten wouldn't be allowed to leave
his mother until it was seven or eight
weeks old, anyway. They had to

give the kittens the chance to learn everything they needed from Tiggy. So she had plenty of time to read the whole book *and* persuade her mum that the tabby kitten would be the perfect pet.

The first time she went, Emma just sat quietly by the door. Tiggy watched her suspiciously, her ears laid back and the tip of her fluffy tail twitching. It was obvious that she was making Tiggy nervous, but she had to get to know the kittens, Emma told herself. It was so important. She wrapped her arms round her knees and just sat listening to the squeaks and rustles in the straw. By the time Dad came to pick her up, Tiggy was lying down feeding the kittens as if Emma wasn't there.

On her next visit, Emma decided to bring Tiggy some cat treats. If Tiggy was distracted, she might let Emma near the kittens. Liz had told her that Tiggy had licked the bowl of fish spotlessly clean, so Emma decided to get fish-flavoured ones.

She crouched down a little way from the kittens and shook some treats out of the packet next to Tiggy. The cat sniffed at them curiously. Emma could tell she wanted the fishy treats, but that

she wasn't ready to eat in front of her.
Emma sat with her chin on her knees,
looking away from Tiggy. Out of the
corner of her eye, she could just see her
edging closer to the pile.

Tiggy made one last little hop and
started to gobble down the treats.
Then she sniffed cautiously at Emma's
right foot – the part of her that was
nearest – and darted back to her
kittens. Emma couldn't stop herself
beaming. It felt like a breakthrough.

She opened the packet again,
making sure that Tiggy could hear it
rustle. Then she wriggled a bit closer,
shaking out a few more treats right
next to the cat. Emma really wanted to
get a proper look at the kittens, as she
thought they must be just over a week

old by now. She was hoping that their eyes would be open. Her cat book said that the kittens would all have blue eyes to begin with.

"They're definitely bigger," Emma whispered to Tiggy, who was still eating the treats. "They're beautiful." Tiggy looked up at Emma with her ears laid back, and Emma sighed. "I know you don't like me talking. I don't want to scare you. I just want them to get used to hearing my voice. Anybody's voice, really."

Tiggy crunched the last fishy biscuit, and Emma took a deep breath. She had stroked the cat a couple of times before, but not since she'd had the kittens. Slowly, she held out her hand to let Tiggy sniff it.

Tiggy dabbed her nose at Emma's hand cautiously, but she didn't hiss or raise the fur on her back. She actually looked quite calm. She rubbed her chin along Emma's wrist, and then strolled back towards the kittens.

Emma held her breath and put the same hand down in the straw, next to the kittens. Tiggy lay down, stretched out beside her babies, and Emma smiled delightedly. She was almost touching them! And the little tabby was right next to her hand. Emma wondered if he could smell the fishy treats, too, but she thought he was probably a bit young for that. His eyes were definitely open, though – just tiny blue slits. He looked like a teddy bear, with his round face and little triangle ears.

"I'm so lucky," Emma whispered, "getting to know you now when you're so small."

The kitten mewed squeakily and waved his front paws, wriggling closer to Emma. "I'm not your mum, small puss," she whispered. "I think you want to be over there. For some milk." Very gently she scooped him closer to Tiggy, so he could latch on and suckle. His fur was the softest thing she'd ever felt.

"I've got to think of a name," Emma muttered. "I can't keep just calling you small puss. Sam maybe? Or Sammy... You look like a Sammy. My little Sammy cat."

As the weeks went by, Sammy and the other kittens grew amazingly quickly. By four weeks they could all walk properly, and suddenly they seemed to be interested in everything.

Tiggy spent a lot of her time trying to herd them back together, hurrying round them in the scattered straw and shooing them back to the nest. But as soon as she had one kitten safely tucked away, the other two would be padding out to explore again. Emma thought that Tiggy looked very tired. Liz had been putting down lots more food for her than usual, and Emma had been bringing her bowls of special cat milk and extra snacks, but it was hard work herding kittens and feeding them, too.

The kittens were more like mini cats now – their heads still seemed much too big for their little bodies, but they'd lost their furry balloon look. They were really growing up.

"Hello," Emma whispered, crouching down by the door of the stall. Three little heads popped up at once, and she giggled. They looked so funny, like the meerkats she'd seen at the zoo. Almost at once the tabby kitten plunged over the edge of the straw nest to come and see her.

"I've got something really special for you," Emma murmured. She and Liz had been talking about how they were going to wean the kittens – to get them eating food as well as Tiggy's milk. Emma had looked it up in her book, and Mum had got some baby rice and evaporated milk from the supermarket to mix up for the kittens. It looked a big disgusting, but then Emma didn't much like the look of normal cat food, either.

She'd bought a special litter tray as well, to put in the corner of the stall. According to her book, now that the kittens were trying solid food, they were going to poo a lot more, too. Until now Liz had just scooped out the dirty straw every day.

Liz had said she'd be able to do most of the feeds and cleaning, and Alex and Sarah, who also taught at the stables, had said they could help as well. The kittens were going to need a bowl four times a day, so it was lucky Liz and the others were around.

"This is going to be yummy," Emma promised, dipping her finger in the white goo and holding it out to Sammy.

Sammy sniffed curiously, and Emma rubbed the goo on his nose. He stepped back in surprise and sneezed. Then he licked at the dribbles of baby rice that were running down his muzzle. It was good! He licked harder, running his bright pink tongue all round his mouth and nose.

Sammy padded closer to the girl, hoping for some more of the white stuff. Emma was holding another splodge out for him, and he licked it straight off her finger this time, trying to gobble it up fast. He could hear his brother and sister coming up behind him, and he didn't want to share.

"Look," Emma murmured. "There's a whole bowlful…"

Sammy sniffed hopefully at the bowl, and then started to lap hurriedly. The other two kittens appeared beside him, and his sister plunged her face into the bowl eagerly. She came up smeared in white milky stuff, dripping from her nose and her black whiskers.

The girl laughed, and all the kittens jumped, staring at her nervously.

"Sorry," she whispered softly.

Sammy watched her for a moment, then decided that she didn't mean any harm and went back to lapping. The food was so tasty, but it was making him sleepy, just like feeding from his mother did sometimes. He licked at the last smears at the bottom of the bowl, and then licked his whiskers and yawned.

His brother and sister began to pad back towards their mother, to sleep curled up next to her, but the nest in the straw was a long way away. Sammy yawned again and eyed the girl. She was warm, too – he knew it from the times she'd stroked him. He walked towards her, wobbling a bit, and tried to climb up her leg.

Emma looked at him, smiling in delighted surprise. Then she gently scooped a hand underneath his bottom and lifted him up on to her lap. Sammy flopped down, full and sleepy, and began a tiny purr.

"Oh, Emma," Mum whispered from the doorway. "Is that Sammy? You said it was the tabby one you really liked."

"Yes," Emma breathed. "He fell asleep on me. And he was purring, Mum."

"He is gorgeous," Mum said, smiling. "What does Tiggy think about him sleeping on you?"

Emma giggled. "She's asleep, too.

I think she's grateful! She must be worn out looking after them all. I need to ask Liz if she's got something we can put across the doorway of the stall, a plank of wood maybe. So that Tiggy can get out, but the kittens won't. Otherwise they'll be wandering all over the place soon. We might never find them!" She sighed. "I suppose we have to go, don't we?"

"We can hang on for a little bit. I don't want to make you move him. Why don't I go and ask Liz about finding something for the door?"

Emma nodded. Then, as her mum was turning to leave, she suddenly whispered, "Mum!"

"What is it? Is he waking up after all?"

"No, it's just … do you think we could adopt him? You said we had to see about having one of Tiggy's kittens – in case they were too wild."

Her mum looked down at Sammy, stretched out blissfully on Emma's knee. "He doesn't look very wild, does he?"

Emma shook her head, beaming.

Mum smiled at her. "All right then, we can adopt him. I'll tell Liz now."

Chapter Five

Keira stood by the door of the stall, looking cautiously round it at Tiggy and the dancing kittens. Emma had managed to persuade her to come and see them at last. They were playing with a toy that Emma had bought – a bundle of feathers on the end of a long wire that she could flick and wave about. The kittens loved it.

They stalked it, pounced on it, bounced around it, and all the while Tiggy sat watching them proudly. Every so often she couldn't resist and put out a paw to dab at the feathers, too.

"They're so funny," Keira whispered to Emma. "I wish…"

"You could have a go," Emma suggested, holding out the toy.

Keira shook her head. "No," she said quickly. "It's OK."

Emma wanted to persuade her, but she had a feeling it would only make Keira feel worse. "I want to wear Sammy out a bit, before Dad comes and we put him in the carrying box," she explained. Dad was bringing the box when he came to pick Emma up from her lesson, any time now.

"Do you think Sammy won't like it?" Keira asked.

"I don't know." Emma sighed. "It feels mean taking him away from Tiggy and the other kittens, but he's about nine weeks old. Lots of kittens go to new homes then, even though it's a bit young. From the websites Dad and I looked at it sounded like it'd be best to rehome Sammy as soon as possible. Otherwise he'll do whatever his mum does. Tiggy still doesn't really like being touched, and she'd never let me pick her up. I don't want Sammy to learn to be scared of people from her."

"What's going to happen to the other kittens?" Keira asked.

"Liz thinks she's found a lady who wants them," Emma said happily. "She's had cats before and she's going to take them both together. Later this week, I think." She glanced anxiously at Tiggy, who was still watching her kittens closely. "Poor Tiggy, she'll really miss them. But it is the best thing for the kittens, I'm sure it is."

"Oh! Your dad's here," Keira said, turning to look out of the barn door.

Emma let out an excited gasp. "Oh, wow..." she murmured. "I'm actually getting to take you home, Sammy!"

She had brought along a packet of cat treats, so they could tempt Sammy into the crate. The kittens were eating dry food like Tiggy now, although theirs was made for kittens. The cat treats were a special extra. Emma took the carrier from her dad and opened the wire door. Then she scattered a few treats inside. Tiggy and all the kittens edged closer – they knew what that rustling noise meant.

"They're all coming," Emma said worriedly to Dad.

"That's probably not a bad thing. We want Sammy to think the box isn't scary. If they all play around in it for a bit, he won't mind going in, will he?"

"I guess not." Emma watched as all three kittens explored their way around the carrier, nibbling at the treats and sniffing the soft cushion lining. Even Tiggy snapped up a treat that was just by the door.

"Emma, look," Dad murmured, a few minutes later. "Sammy's going in on his own. You can close the door in a second."

Emma nodded, and as the white tip of Sammy's striped tail cleared

the door, she gently swung it shut
and twisted the catches.

"Let's go home," she whispered.

Sammy sat pressed against the back
of the box. He had no idea what was
happening – he'd never seen anywhere
but the barn. Now he was shut into the
small, shadowy carrier, and somehow
it was moving. The smells were strange
and sharp, and there was so much noise.
The vibration of the car was completely
new to Sammy and very frightening.

He could hear Emma's voice, and
her dad's, and he knew that they were
familiar, but it wasn't making him feel
much better.

"Do you think he's all right? I thought he might meow, but he's not even making any noise."

"It's a big shock for him, poor kitten. We're nearly back, Emma."

"We're almost home," Emma whispered through the holes in the carrier. "Not much longer."

Sammy felt himself pressed against the side of the carrier as the car swung round a corner. He let out a little hiss of fright and tried to back further into the box – but there wasn't anywhere to go. He scratched at the plastic, just a faint little movement of his paw. Nothing happened. Sammy closed his eyes and hoped his mother would come.

"I don't understand," Emma whispered. "He was so friendly before. He let me pick him up. He even slept on my lap."

"One of those websites did say to expect a kitten to take a couple of steps backwards when it's moved, Ems," Dad pointed out. "He's only been here a few hours."

"I didn't think he'd be this jumpy." Mum looked worriedly at Sammy, tense and nervous, his whiskers bristling.

"He's just a bit scared," Dad said encouragingly.

"I suppose so…" Mum sighed.

Emma looked over at the big wire crate they'd borrowed from one of the neighbours, whose puppy didn't need it any more. Sammy couldn't be loose in the house just yet, as he'd probably run off and hide. But they could put the crate on the table in the corner of the kitchen, and he could see everything that was going on and get used to lots of people being around. The kitchen didn't have any holes a kitten could get stuck in when they let him out to play.

It had seemed like the perfect plan for an almost-wild kitten. But Emma had imagined Sammy watching curiously as she ate her breakfast or did her homework. She'd thought of him purring to Dad as he made the dinner. She hadn't seen a hissing, spitting, miserable little kitten hiding at the back of his crate. He'd even swiped at her with his claws when she put a bowl of fresh water in for him. He'd missed, but still. It was like Sammy was a different kitten.

"We need to give him time," Dad said gently. "A day or so to calm down, before we start trying to handle him again."

"Yes," Emma sighed. "And I know I should have expected he wouldn't be very happy…" But she hadn't thought it would be like this. Mum looked so worried – and she'd really been coming round to the idea of a kitten!

What if she changed her mind?

Dad patted Emma's shoulder, and then gave Mum a hug. "Don't look so tragic, you two! It'll be OK! I'm just going to make some coffee. Do you want anything, Emma?"

Emma shook her head. Deep down, she realized sadly, she'd just thought that Sammy would see how nice their house was. He'd know how excited she was to have a kitten of her own – he'd understand, and he'd settle in straightaway.

"I was being stupid," Emma muttered to herself. She crouched down in front of the crate, looking at Sammy sideways. He was still huddled up at the back, his ears flat against his little head. "I thought everything would be perfect all at once. But I'll do anything to make you love us, Sammy. I just want you to be happy."

Chapter Six

Emma held out her fingers to Sammy. They were covered in roast chicken dinner baby food, which apparently was the most popular flavour with kittens. It felt sticky and gloopy, but she didn't mind. They'd given Sammy a whole twenty-four hours to calm down, and Emma just couldn't wait any more. All the websites said that

the way to make a half-wild kitten
like you was to use food. They had to
make Sammy see that food came from
people, and if he wanted the food he
had to put up with them, too.

"He's noticed, Ems," Dad breathed
behind her. "He can smell it."

It was true. Emma could see
Sammy's ears flickering, just a little.
And his eyes were widening. "He must
be able to smell it," she murmured.
"It smells *disgusting*."

"Not to a cat," Dad whispered back.

"He's coming!" Emma tried not to
sound too excited, or too loud. Sammy
was stepping delicately, cautiously
across the crate to sniff at her fingers.
His tiny pink tongue flicked out, and
he began to lick them.

Emma held her face straight, trying not to laugh and scare him away, but it tickled so much. His tongue was very strong for such a small kitten. And it was so rough. Emma leaned a little closer, so she could see the tiny white hairs all over his tongue. Sammy stopped licking and glanced worriedly up at her for a second. But then the deliciousness of the baby food won, and he went back to getting every last bit out from under Emma's fingernails.

Emma wanted to pull her hand away to get some more from the jar, but she was sure that would frighten Sammy. Then she rolled her eyes. Of course! She dipped her other hand in, lifting out several fat fingerfuls, and slowly moved that hand into the crate, too.

Sammy moved his head from side to side, as though he wasn't sure which hand to go for.

"Aww, poor Sammy – you've confused him now," Dad said.

Sammy decided that he couldn't get much more from Emma's right hand and changed to gulping down the food from her left. Emma looked at him thoughtfully. Her right hand was still in the crate. Very gently, she ran her hand down Sammy's back. He tensed a little, but he didn't spring away. Emma kept softly stroking his fur.

"Is that nice?" she whispered. "Is it nice being stroked, mmm?"

Sammy glanced up at her, as if to check what the noise was, but he kept licking.

"Keep stroking him," Dad murmured. "I'm going to get a little bowl of his proper dry food. Let's see if we can get him to eat that with us still here watching him."

He filled the bowl quietly and passed it to Emma so she could put it in front of Sammy. The little kitten darted back as the bowl suddenly appeared, but then he caught the scent of the dry cat food he was used to. He gave Emma's fingers one last hopeful swipe with his tongue and moved on to the bowl.

"You try stroking him," Emma whispered to Dad.

Dad nodded and reached slowly into the crate, running one finger down Sammy's back as he busily gobbled the food. Sammy glanced over his shoulder, but he didn't stop eating.

"It really works," Dad murmured. "We can do this again when we feed him at lunchtime."

Emma nodded. "Every time we feed him. And maybe soon we can get him out of the crate and let him eat from his bowl on the floor." She sighed happily. "It's really going to be OK, Dad, I'm sure it is."

"Which top do you think I should wear?" Mum held two out on hangers.

"Mmm. The black one," Emma said, watching Sammy. He'd nearly finished his bowl of food and he was looking sleepy. She had her arm inside his cage, with her hand cupped round him. Emma had a feeling he might fall asleep with her hand still there, which would be brilliant. He'd be almost back to the same friendly Sammy she'd known at the stables, and it was only a week since they'd brought him home.

"Are you sure?" Mum frowned. "You didn't look for very long…"

"Yes, Mum. I can stroke Sammy *and* look, you know. Hurry up! Auntie Grace'll be here to babysit soon."

Mum rushed off, and Emma giggled and gently moved the food bowl. Sammy had fallen asleep with his head in it! He twitched a little and then flopped down, collapsing across her hand with a little wheezy snore. She leaned against the crate, closing her eyes and smiling dreamily to herself. Soon they'd be able to take him out of there and he'd be a real pet, she was sure.

"Are you asleep, Emma?"

"Oh! Auntie Grace, shh. I'm not, but Sammy is." Emma reached out the arm that wasn't in the crate to hug her aunt. "I didn't hear you come in."

"Your dad was walking up the path when I pulled up, so I didn't have to ring the bell. He's just gone to change. So this is Sammy? He's gorgeous."

"Isn't he?" Emma agreed proudly. "And he's getting much more confident again. He was really upset on Saturday when we brought him home, but he's a lot happier now." Carefully, she slid her hand out from underneath him, and Sammy snuffled but stayed asleep. She grinned at her aunt. "I've got pins and needles now. Mum says please can you help me

with my science homework, but she's
got us a DVD for afterwards."

Emma yawned and snuggled against
Auntie Grace. "Can't we watch a bit
more?"

"No! You know your mum said
eight-thirty, cheeky. Besides, haven't
you got to feed Sammy before bed?"

"Oh yes, and you haven't seen him
awake yet, I forgot!" Emma sprang
up from the sofa. "I'll go and get his
food." She hurried into the kitchen
and began to measure it out, while
Sammy padded up and down the crate,
watching her and mewing hopefully.

Emma had just opened the door

of the crate to put the bowl in when
Auntie Grace pushed open the kitchen
door. It banged slightly, and Sammy
jumped at the noise. He saw Auntie
Grace – someone he'd never met
before – and suddenly panicked. He
hissed loudly, and Emma stared at
him. "What's the matter, Sammy?"

"Oh dear, is he OK?" Auntie Grace
asked, leaning over to look at him.

Sammy hissed again as he saw the
strange person coming closer. He
darted out of the crate door, desperate
to get away.

"I think he's a bit scared because
you're new," Emma said worriedly,
trying to catch him. "Maybe you'd
better just let me sort him out, Auntie
Grace."

Auntie Grace stepped back out of the kitchen, but Sammy was already spooked. He scrabbled over Emma's arm in a panic, accidentally clawing at her wrist so that she squeaked and dropped the food bowl.

The bowl smashed on the tiles with a huge crash, and Sammy yowled in fright. He raced round the side of the crate, but the table was pushed up against the wall below the window and there was nowhere to go. Frantically, he clawed his way up the curtains, digging his tiny claws into the fabric.

Sammy hung there, swaying a little. He didn't really understand what had happened. He'd been about to eat his food – he could smell it – and then suddenly everything was different and terrifying. Now he didn't even know where he was, or how he'd got so high up.

The curtain fabric ripped a little under his weight, and he slid down a few centimetres with a frightened mew. He tried to claw his way back up again, but the shiny fabric was difficult to climb, and he slipped further down.

"Sammy, it's all right..." Emma's voice, low and soothing. And now he wasn't falling any more. Her hands were around him, the way they were when she fed him sometimes. After struggling for a moment, he let her unhook his paws from the few last threads of the curtains, and sat tensely in her hands, ears back and fur fluffed up. She lifted him down, still whispering gently, and slid him back into the crate. Sammy backed away from the door anxiously, but the strange person had gone now, he could see. It was just Emma. He knew her. She was safe.

Chapter Seven

"Emma! You're still up!"

Emma jerked awake. Mum was standing in the living-room doorway, looking surprised.

"Sorry," said Auntie Grace. "Emma was upset, I didn't want to make her go to bed…"

"What happened?" Dad asked, just at the same time as Mum noticed

Emma's scratched wrist and swooped down to check it.

"Emma, you've hurt yourself! Oh no, was it Sammy?"

"He didn't mean to." Emma looked sleepily at Dad and Mum. "It was an accident. And, um, I broke his food bowl. Sorry… We swept it up."

"What's been going on?" Dad sat down on the arm of the sofa, and Mum came to sit next to Emma.

Emma sighed. She was so tired it was hard to explain. "I went to feed him, but he was scared of Auntie Grace."

"It was my fault. I should have thought, of course, he's never seen me before," Auntie Grace put in. "And he's a bit more nervous than most kittens. I frightened him and he jumped out of the crate and scratched Emma by accident."

"And that made me drop his bowl, and he got even more scared and ran up the curtains."

"Oh my goodness," Mum muttered.

"I'm afraid he did tear them a bit," Auntie Grace went on slowly. "But he's back in the crate now and he's calmed down. In fact, last time Emma checked he was asleep, wasn't he?"

Emma nodded.

Mum leaned back against the sofa and let out a huge sigh. "I knew this was a mistake. We should never have brought him home. He was so upset when we took him away from the stables and his mum. I just don't think it's fair."

"Mum!" Emma gasped.

"Oh, Emma. You have to see I'm right – just look at your wrist!"

Emma looked down at the three long red lines, and the little scratches that she'd got all over her hands when she was taking Sammy off the curtains. They were sore, but it hadn't been Sammy's fault. He was just scared – he hadn't meant to hurt her.

Mum put her arm round Emma. "I know how hard you've tried with Sammy, but he might not be the right cat for us after all. He needs to go to a shelter, I think. Where they've got people who are used to looking after cats like him."

"I'm not sure," Dad said. "I know Sammy was difficult when we brought him home, but he is getting better."

"Getting better!" Mum stared at him. "Emma's covered in scratches!"

"I don't think it's that big a deal," Auntie Grace said gently. "Even Whisky scratches me sometimes, if I go to pick him up and he just doesn't feel like it."

Mum sighed again. "I'm sorry, Emma, but he's too unpredictable. I'm not sure he's ever going to be really friendly. Maybe he needs a home more like the stables, where he doesn't have to be around people if he doesn't want to."

"Mum, please don't send him away!" Emma wailed. "I don't want any other cat, only Sammy! He'll be fine, he will. I'll do anything to keep him." She stared pleadingly at her mum, tears trickling down her cheeks. She couldn't bear the thought of poor Sammy going to a shelter – somewhere else strange and new and frightening. He'd have to start all over again, and soon it would be too late to tame him. He'd be shy and wild forever.

"Look, just give us a few more weeks, love," Dad suggested. "Of course today's a bit of a setback, but we have to keep trying."

"Two more weeks." Mum looked from Emma to Dad and back again. "We have to be able to tell by then, don't we?"

Dad nodded slowly. "All right. Emma?"

"I suppose so," Emma whispered huskily. She was so upset her voice seemed to have disappeared. Two weeks! It was no time at all.

"What's the matter?" Keira asked, as she led Jasmine past Emma and Sparky. "Is Sparky being a pain about getting tacked up again? You look, well, a bit sad..." she trailed off, not sure what to say. Emma looked like she might be about to cry.

"No." Emma sniffed. "Actually Sparky's been a total star. Maybe he can tell I just can't deal with a tricksy pony today."

"Oh no, what is it?" Keira swapped Jasmine's reins to her other hand and gave Emma a hug. "Don't cry!"

"I can't help it." Emma's voice shook. "Mum says we might have to give Sammy to a shelter. She thinks we can't cope with him."

"But wasn't it going really well?" Keira said, confused. "You showed me that photo your dad took of him eating off your fingers. He looked so happy."

"He's still jumpy, though," Emma gulped. "Mum thinks he's not going to adapt to living in a house. He got scared last night because my auntie was there

102

and he scratched me. I didn't mind –
not much – but Mum was really upset
about it. She says we've got two weeks
to prove he can be a proper pet, or he
has to go." She could hardly get the last
words out, she was crying so much.

Keira hugged her tighter, and even
Sparky and Jasmine leaned in close, as if
they wanted to make Emma feel better.

"Two weeks is a long time," Keira said. "Honestly, it really is. And I saw how friendly and tame he was with you here. You nearly had *me* stroking him, Emma, and I'm scared of cats!"

"I suppose so…" Emma said, between gasps. "It doesn't feel like long, though. If he goes to a shelter he'll be all lost and alone. It'll be awful."

"Then you absolutely have to make sure it doesn't happen," Keira said firmly. "I'll see if I can think of anything to help." She gave Emma one last hug. "Ems, we have to go. Liz is waving at us. She wants us to try those dressage aids today, remember?"

Emma nodded and sniffed hard. "I'm OK. I'm so glad I told you about it, Keira. I do actually feel a bit happier."

Emma grabbed her riding hat from
the back seat and looked anxiously
at Auntie Grace's purple car parked
outside their house.

"It's all right," Dad said soothingly.
"She said she wouldn't go near Sammy.
Although we will have to try and
get him used to meeting new people
eventually. She's got something for
you."

Emma hurried down the path,
curious to see what Auntie Grace
had brought. She had a feeling it was
something important – not just a
magazine or some chocolate to cheer
her up, but something that really
mattered.

"Emma! I'm so glad you got back before I had to go to work. Look, I've brought you this." Auntie Grace whirled out of the front door on to the path. "Here. I really hope it helps."

Emma looked down at the book that her aunt had pressed into her hands – *Taming Feral Kittens*. There was a gorgeous little ginger kitten on the front of it, with a shy, worried look on his face that made Emma think of Sammy at once.

"I got it at the animal shelter. I thought I'd go and ask them if they had any tips for you. They were so friendly and helpful. This was written by someone who used to work there, and they said to call if you get really stuck. I wrote the number inside the cover for you." She hugged Emma. "Sweetheart, if Sammy does have to go there, they will look after him, I promise."

Emma nodded. "But it's not going to happen," she said firmly. "This is brilliant, Auntie Grace. I'm going to go and read it now."

Sammy sat in the doorway of the crate, looking out suspiciously. Everything was different – the crate had been moved down on to the floor, and he didn't like that, for a start. He preferred to be high up, so he could see who was coming. High up was safe.

But he liked the open door. He thought he did, anyway. He sniffed the air beyond the crate, his whiskers twitching. He could step out, right on to the floor. He could explore. Cautiously, he extended one paw over the door frame, and then the next, and then his two back paws.

He stood nervously just outside the crate, watching, scanning the room. Emma was there, sitting in the corner, and her dad was over by the counter. She wasn't looking at him – she was gazing off into the distance as if she hadn't noticed what he was doing. Sammy took a few steps out into the room and sniffed.

Food! He could definitely smell food. He was sure it was well past his usual feeding time. He'd been expecting Emma to bring food, but instead she and her dad had lifted his crate down on to the floor. Determinedly, he stomped across the floor, towards the smell. Emma had his bowl on her lap. He stopped a few steps away from her, looking uncertainly at the bowl. He wasn't sure he wanted to go any closer, but he was hungry.

His tail swished from side to side, and then he made a panicked little run, flinging himself at the bowl. What if she took it away? Sammy climbed up on Emma's leg and started to gobble down the food as quickly as he could.

"It's all right," Emma murmured. "I'm not going anywhere."

Sammy's ears flickered, but he didn't stop eating. Then he felt her stroking him, very gently running her hand over his shoulders and down his back. It was nice – it felt like his mother licking him. He slowed his eating down a little, almost sure that the bowl wasn't going to be taken away.

At last, he'd finished the whole bowl. He licked round it carefully and then sniffed it to make sure there wasn't any more. There wasn't, but he was full anyway.

Slowly, carefully, he settled down
into a crouch on Emma's lap. She was
still stroking him, so gently. Sammy
stretched out his paws and kneaded
them up and down on Emma's skirt.
Then he closed his eyes and purred.

Chapter Eight

Emma tucked the phone under her chin so she could talk to Auntie Grace and have both hands free for scrabbling after the ping-pong ball as Sammy sent it skittering around all over the floor.

"It really works," she told her aunt, a little breathlessly. "We started on Sunday after I'd had time to read the book. All this week, we've only fed him with the bowl on me or Dad, so that he has to come to us to get his food. And he's always hungry, so it works perfectly. The very first time we tried it, he let me stroke him and he even purred! I'm starting to think he actually does like me," she added shyly.

"Of course he does. Oh, that's wonderful, Emma! I felt awful when your mum said you might have to give him up."

"Me, too. But I'm so hoping she's going to let me keep him. She was laughing at him this morning, when he was playing with his feathery toy before school. He kept almost falling over backwards, he was trying so hard to catch it." Emma threw the ping-pong ball again for Sammy. "We're doing the next thing it says in the book now. He's going to be allowed out in the kitchen all the time, not just for food time and playing. His bed and his litter tray are still in the crate, but we'll leave it open so he can come and go when he wants to."

"And then I suppose you'll bring his bed out, and eventually get rid of the crate?"

"Exactly. I don't know how long it's going to take, though. The book says it depends on the kitten. Oh, Sammy!"

"What did he do?" Auntie Grace laughed at the other end of the line.

"He chased after the ball so fast he ran into the cupboard. He's fine, he just looks a bit confused. One minute." Emma laid the phone on the floor and wriggled closer to Sammy, murmuring comforting noises. She was sure that he looked embarrassed, if a kitten could. His ears had gone flat.

"It's OK," she whispered and without thinking about it, she scooped Sammy gently into her hands and snuggled him up against her cardigan. "Oh… I didn't mean to…" It was the first time she'd ever picked him up. But Sammy hadn't clawed her, or jumped away in fright. He was huddled against her, so tiny and fragile that she could feel his heart beating under her fingers. "You don't mind?" she murmured. "Oh, Sammy, I do love you…"

"Hey…" Dad whispered from the doorway. "He looks happy!"

"Dad, can you pick up the phone?"

Emma whispered. "I was talking to
Auntie Grace. She must be wondering
what happened to me. Can you tell
her I'll call her later?"

Dad chuckled. "Sure. I'll tell her
you're occupied with some very
important business."

"Are you sure?" Emma looked worriedly at Keira. "I mean, I'd love it if you came over for lunch. But I know how you feel about cats."

"Exactly," Keira called back, as she hefted Jasmine's saddle over to the tackroom. "And so does your mum. So if even silly Keira isn't scared of playing with Sammy, he must be OK as a pet, mustn't he? The two weeks are up, aren't they? We need to show your mum how good Sammy is."

"Two weeks yesterday. I haven't wanted to ask Mum what's happening." Emma sighed. "And I never said you were silly," she added quickly.

Keira grinned. "I know. But I am silly.

I can't even say what it is that makes me frightened of cats. They just make me so nervous."

"I don't want you to be miserable." Emma frowned. "And…" She nibbled her bottom lip. "If you're nervous it might make Sammy nervous, too," she explained. "He was all right with Auntie Grace when she came over in the week. She was really good, she just sat on the floor completely still until he was brave enough to sniff at her. But she's used to cats and she wasn't scared."

"I won't be scared, either," Keira said. "I promise. I said I'd try to think of something I could do to help, and this is it. I'll be brave." She smiled at Emma. "Honestly. I'll be fine."

"He's in here, in the kitchen." Emma looked back at Keira. She could see her mum hovering behind her friend, with an anxious expression on her face. Mum obviously wasn't sure about this – neither was Emma, to be honest. But Keira seemed so certain. She'd explained to Emma's mum in the car that she wanted to try and stop being scared of cats, and that she knew she'd be OK with Sammy because he was so little.

Emma opened the door slowly and peered round. "Oh, he's asleep in his basket. Actually, that's good. How about we sit on the floor for a bit? We can have a snack, and then when he

wakes up we can let him come and
see you."

Keira nodded. She was quite pale,
Emma thought. But she looked
determined, too. "That's a good idea."

Emma took her hand, pulling her
gently into the kitchen to sit down
half under the table. That would give
Sammy plenty of space to look at
them properly before he got out of
his basket. Keira even giggled when
Emma's mum handed them a plate of
cheese cubes and apple to eat under
there. "It's like being really small and
making tents under the table. Did you
ever do that?" she whispered.

"Yes! Hey, I think he's waking up."
Emma glanced at her. "Sure you're
all right?"

"Mm-hm."

Emma could feel Keira tensing up beside her. Maybe it *was* a stupid idea, after all. But it was too late to do anything about it now.

Sammy stretched and yawned, and popped his head up out of his basket to see what was happening. He was hungry and he could smell something delicious. Not his normal food, but that only made it more exciting. He twitched his ears forward and gazed at Emma under the table. Emma and someone else. He flicked his tail from side to side worriedly. It wasn't someone he knew, but she was sitting quite still. She had some of whatever it was that smelled so nice, he could see it in her hands. And she was holding it very close to the floor…

Sammy hopped out of his basket and set off across the floor, his whiskers trembling as he smelled the cheese. He nudged his head against

Emma's feet on the way, as if to say
that she belonged to him. But he was
still more interested in the cheese. He
padded between Emma's legs and the
new girl's, and sniffed hopefully at the
girl's fingers. She was holding that
piece of cheese as if she didn't really
want it at all.

He froze for a second,
ears flickering, expecting
someone to shoo him
away. But no one did.
Swiftly, Sammy
swooped the scrap
out of her hand
and gulped
it down,
savouring
every crumb.

Then he licked Keira's fingers, just to check he hadn't missed any. He felt her laugh – her fingers shook – but there was no more cheese. He gave her one last lick, and turned to scramble up into Emma's lap. He could still smell cheese, and he was sure that if Emma had any, she'd give it to him. He hauled himself up her leggings, breathing hard, and half fell into her lap. Then he sat there and gave a massive yawn, showing all his tiny sharp teeth and his raspberry-pink tongue.

"He's gorgeous," Keira whispered, sounding quite surprised.

"You didn't mind when he licked you?" Emma asked. She couldn't stop smiling – Sammy had perched himself on her lap like he belonged.

Keira wrinkled her nose. "Actually, I was really scared. But he's so little – I just kept thinking I could run out if I couldn't deal with it."

"Oh, Keira," Emma's mum murmured. "Do you want to go into the other room?"

Keira shook her head. "No, I think it's OK," she said cautiously. "He's really good."

Emma's mum nodded. "I suppose he is." She smiled at Emma. "So, are you having lunch under the table, then?"

"I don't think we'd actually get much of our lunch if we did that." Slowly, carefully, Emma moved on to her knees, cuddling Sammy against her fleece top as she stood up and went to sit on one of the kitchen chairs. She was waiting for him to leap away, but Sammy only stretched his neck out so he could peer over the edge of the table at the plate of sandwiches that her mum was putting down.

Keira laughed. "He's eyeing the food as though you never feed him, Emma."

"He needn't think he's making a habit of sitting on your lap at mealtimes," Mum said sternly. "Just this once."

Emma stared at her delightedly. "You mean…"

Her mum nodded. "Yes – I was talking to your dad about it last night. Sammy's so much happier now. Oh, Emma, watch out, he's going for that ham sandwich!" She quickly pulled the plate back, and Sammy looked disappointed.

"I'll get you a bit in a minute," Emma whispered in his ear. "A whole sandwich, if you like!"

Sammy yawned again and purred a little and rubbed his face against her hand. Then he nuzzled at Emma's top, and pawed his way gently over the zip, snuggling down inside.

Emma looked down lovingly at the little tabby kitten curled up inside her fleece. "Sammy, you're staying!"